ECHOES FROM THE PAST

A YOUNG MAN'S SEARCH FOR LOVE AND IDENTITY

Published by Revival Waves of Glory
Books & Publishing

PO Box 596 | Litchfield, Illinois 62056 USA

www.revivalwavesofgloryministries.com

Revival Waves of Glory Books & Publishing is committed to excellence in the publishing industry.

Published in the United States of America

Library of Congress Control Number: 2016921477

Revival Waves of Glory, Litchfield, ILLINOIS

Paperback: 978-1-62676-901-4

Hardcover: 978-1-68411-196-1

ECHOES FROM THE PAST

A YOUNG MAN'S SEARCH
FOR LOVE AND IDENTITY

MOBONI LEWIS

CHAPTER 1

My Childhood

RJ and I were very close. He was the father I never had and I was one of the many "sons" with whom he surrounded himself.

You see, my real dad, Brian, left when I was two years old, according to my mother, Lorna. They'd been childhood sweethearts, or so she thought. But Brian—being very adventurous—soon left mum for the thrill.

Rick Doe, my step dad, wasn't much of a father to me. He was always very angry and often times very violent. Mum said it was because he'd had a very difficult childhood.

I came back from school one afternoon to find mum crying. She'd been beaten black and blue by Rick for expressing a desire to find my dad. I ran over to mum almost immediately; a part of me felt responsible for her pain, but Rick asked me to stay away. I was being shipped off to Aunt Becca, my mum's older sister, who lived several miles away. No explanations were given, except that I was no longer a part of the family. I wept sore. I was only seven.

That evening, Rick dropped me off at the train station and handed me over to some guard, then left without a word. I banged on the train window as it pulled out of the platform, crying for mum and wondering if I'd ever see her again.

The train journey lasted over six hours and by the time we arrived in Vey, where Aunt Becca lived, I could hardly walk. Rick hadn't paid the full fares, so I had to sit in the luggage compartment with my legs up for the entire journey.

The guard was very nice and gave me some sandwiches and a glass of milk. He told me he had a little boy named Simon. I sat there wondering if Simon had a kind face like his Dad.

Half an hour later, Aunt Becca arrived in her blue Volkswagen. I hadn't seen her since I was four but recognized her almost immediately. Her face hadn't changed, but she'd lost a lot of weight and looked much older. "Henry!" She called out, loudly, running towards me and holding out her arms, expecting me to run into them. My legs were still kind of sleepy, so I sauntered towards her, as fast as I could, with my luggage, smiling broadly. I loved Aunt Becca. She'd always been nice to me, but she and mum never saw eye to eye and that was all because of Rick.

Aunt Becca lived in a quaint village of a few hundred people, and her house was very immaculate. Sadly, she lived alone, having promised herself not to remarry after her husband, Bob, died in a car accident. I couldn't help but wonder what her kids, my cousins would have been like, and if we would have been close, but I'll never know. Aunt Becca told me I was going to be staying with her—for as I long as I wanted. Even though I loved her very much, I still would have preferred living with mum.

A few hours later, I was being handed a brown envelope. It was a letter from my dad. Aunt Becca said he'd often dropped by, asking about me and wanting to know how I was.

I read Dad's letter almost immediately, tears filling my eyes. He told me how he'd come back looking for mum and how he'd never wanted to leave us. He also asked me if mum was happy with Rick, and if he treated me well.

I wrote back to Dad that same day, telling him about my new life with Aunt Becca and that Rick had often beaten mum. I also told him that Rick had been very mean to me and that I looked forward to seeing him, Brian, and spending some time with him. I already had my mind on a fishing trip to the huge lake I'd seen on my way to Aunt Becca's, and that night I dreamt about dad, and it was the best dream ever.

The following day, Aunt Becca and I went shopping. My clothes were threadbare and my shoes had holes. I needed new ones for school and for church, Aunt Becca said. "Church?" I asked wide-eyed. I'd never attended a service in my life, but Aunt Becca assured me I was going to be fine. Apparently, the people at church were very friendly and already knew I was coming.

By 6.00 a.m. the following day, Aunt Becca was up, humming and making breakfast, and almost immediately my mind went to mum. Rick had always insisted on having a huge breakfast, so mum was often up at the crack of dawn, cranking up the old smoky gas stove, as Rick took his bath. I could almost hear the kettle whistling and the eggs sizzling. It was the same fry-up every morning: bacon, eggs, and sausages, with beans on toast. And just then I heard Aunt Becca calling my name; breakfast was ready. I ran down the stairs as fast as I could, and to my surprise, the table had been laid, with a lacy white tablecloth. I felt like a king. Aunt Becca said I could eat as much as I wanted, and I did, and then we were off to church.

The church folk welcomed me with open arms, hugging me warmly and asking how I was, and somehow they all seemed to know my name. I later got to know that they'd been praying for me, at Aunt Becca's request. The service went on for longer than I had expected, but the people seemed to enjoy every minute, with spontaneous shouts of praise from an elderly woman called Delores.

Three hours later, we were back home and then Aunt Becca's friends began turning up at the house with all kinds of food. It was Aunt Becca's surprise birthday party. I'd never seen so much food in my life and ended up being sick, having tried a bit of everything.

Aunt Becca insisted that I stay home the following day. She said I needed to regain my strength. Then a letter arrived from mum. She said she missed me and wished she'd been able to come with me. I broke down in tears almost immediately, and that very day, made up my mind to become a policeman, so I could protect her from Rick.

CHAPTER 2

My New School

My first day at Kings Primary school wasn't without its "problems". I was the new kid on the block; some other kids thought it was right to boss me around, making up rules that didn't exist so that I ended up doing stuff I should never have been asked to do. One boy called George Clay made me stand on my desk after school, telling everyone why I had moved school, while one of his friends, Felix Brown said I couldn't leave the class until after everyone else because I was the newbie. I didn't know any better so I simply did as I was told.

I was staying behind one afternoon when one of the teachers came hurrying over. Her name was Mercy Fanny. She'd noticed that I always stayed behind and wondered if I was having problems at home. I told her what Felix had said, and she was very furious, promising to deal with the matter the following day. She kept her promise, but that didn't stop others from playing silly tricks on me. One afternoon, George Clay began having a go at me for going on the swing at recess; "his swing". I cowered in the corner, crying as others began chanting for us to fight.

Suddenly, one little girl badged into the playground, stamping her tiny feet and shaking her equally tiny fist at George. I had no idea who she was, but I could tell that George was afraid of her as he began backing away. By the time I got up, however, the girl was gone, but I soon caught up with her. She was the kindest person I'd ever met. She told me she'd watched the boys taunt me every day and felt she had to help me. I thanked Belinda for coming to my rescue. From then on, Belinda and I became the best of friends.

On getting home that afternoon, a letter was waiting for me from my dad. I'd come to recognize his writing and began jumping up in excitement, but the feeling didn't last; Dad told me that after careful consideration, he'd decided not to visit me so as not to unsettle me, and that broke my heart even more. It was like being rejected a second time.

I wept all afternoon, wondering why my own father would want nothing to do with me, but soon convinced myself that it was probably never meant to be.

CHAPTER 3

Rick and Lorna

In Bedew, Rick and Lorna have been fighting all week. Tired of being punched day and night, Lorna decides to run away, but soon discovers that Rick has transferred all the money from their joint account into his. So, Lorna Doe begins cleaning other people's houses for a living, working from dawn till dusk, and saving up; for a train ticket to Vey and for some decent clothes.

Following Lorna's disappearance, however, Rick Doe begins playing the caring husband, putting up notices in shop windows and telling his clients that his wife had left him, sometimes shedding a tear or two, as he cleverly shows them her photograph.

Some four weeks later, while cleaning in an upmarket area of Bedew, Lorna learns of a live-in nanny post a few kilometres away. She's very excited and puts in an application. Her application is accepted and she's asked to move in, immediately. Lorna turns up for work the following day, to find Rick waiting. Her new employer, Abel Wright, was one of Rick's clients and had set her up.

But that afternoon, as Rick dragged Lorna down the flight of stairs, pulling her hair and spitting in her face, Abel knew he'd made a mistake by turning Lorna in, and was soon calling the police in confidence, and a few days later, Lorna Doe is taken to a safe house several miles away from Bedew and given a new identity among scores of other women, all of whom had been victims of domestic violence.

One year on and with hardly any information on Lorna, Rick decides to go looking for her at Becca's, but he and Becca aren't the best of friends, so he employs the help of his personal assistant, Andrea Bates. Andrea would go looking for Lorna in Vey, pretending to be Lorna's long lost friend, Rita Keys. And so, very early the next day, Andrea Bates sets out for Vey, with nothing but Becca's address.

Arriving in Vey, Andrea knows almost immediately that her work has been cut out. Vey is a very small village and outsiders stand out like a sore thumb. Telling the first few people that her name is Andrea, and then Rita, others soon became suspicious of who she really was, and won't give her any information. But one young man is willing to break the rank, albeit in secret. And so, Andrea is driven around Vey, hunched in the back seat of a minicab, only to be dropped off at the village square. Frustrated, angry, and now out of pocket, Andrea Bates begins trekking the four-mile journey back to the station, and with a promise never to return to the village.

Rick Doe, is, of course, very angry that Andrea has returned to Bedew with no information on Lorna, and soon terminates the young girl's appointment. And with his trusted assistant now out of the picture, Rick's business begins falling apart. Andrea had managed his diary, balanced his books, run his errands; in short, she'd run his life. Rick tries all he can to get Andrea back, but the young girl refuses, and then a few months later, the tax man comes knocking. Rick had been fiddling his figures all these years and Andrea had turned him in.

With that, Rick Doe is put behind bars for twelve years, while his remaining assets are frozen.

CHAPTER 4

My Secondary School

Fast forward five years, I was going to one of the best boarding schools in the county. Thanks to Aunt Becca, her army of tutors had me working my socks off, three hours a day, four days a week, for two years. Looking back now, I wonder how I survived.

Harem Comprehensive Secondary School in Warymore was Aunt Becca's choice. The school had a reputation for turning students into future leaders, it said; in the prospectus, and Aunt Becca was determined that I became one. Moreover, the head teacher, Christopher Dolous, had promised to look out for me if I was accepted. It was the perfect arrangement.

Three weeks later, I was leaving for Harem Comprehensive. Aunt Becca gave me her Bible just as I was about to board the train, having left mine at home. I returned it because she probably needed it more than I did, I thought.

Boarding school was great. I made lots of friends, particularly with older boys as I attempted to fill the void left by my father. There was Dick Singh, Albert May, Julius Enders and Nick Yates, and I soon discovered that we all had one thing in common: none of us had dads. And before long I was being introduced to their "Dad" RJ, a bearded, middle-aged man who lived just outside the school compound. RJ became my "Dad" almost immediately and was soon teaching me how to shave properly, amongst many other things.

I'd only seen Christopher Dolous twice. He was hardly ever available and when he was, he would ask me the same questions over and over as though I was a kid. I doubted if he really cared about me and after a while, I stopped swinging by his office.

But Lorna isn't happy with the decision to send Henry to boarding school and soon accuses Becca of wanting to get rid of the young boy for good. Upset and angry at being slated, Becca Payne cuts off all communication with her younger sister, leaving Lorna in the dark about her son's future.

A few months later, the boys told me we had an outing with RJ. It was the last Saturday of the month and the only time we were allowed out of school. I jumped up in excitement, and almost immediately began thinking of what to wear. This was my chance to show off my threads. And then, of course, RJ was a good cook. His signature burgers often had us munching noisily late into the night as others slept. Spending the day with him would be nothing but one big party, I'd thought to myself.

Some time after 4.00 p.m., we all gathered at RJ's house, and then just before 6.00 p.m., the other boys began changing into hooded tops as RJ mapped out our journey for the evening. I froze and began to panic. RJ gave me a pat on the back, handed me a hooded top, and soon we were on our way.

No one spoke as the van headed down the dusty road. I tried looking into the faces of the other boys, but everyone seemed preoccupied, lost in their own world of only God knows what.

Half an hour later, the van pulled up outside a pub, and one by one the boys jumped out. I was the last to leave the vehicle as my legs had become weak with fear. Nick dragged me out and I landed on my side. He pulled me up with one hand and I had no choice but to stand on my feet, limping along as we filed into the pub.

RJ ordered a round for everyone. Up until then, I had never had a drink in my life but felt obligated to down a shot. I knew I couldn't get through the evening without steadying my nerves. I had a sip and began to cough. The others started laughing, so I downed the remaining liquor, and almost immediately felt bold. I was ready for anything. We stayed at the pub playing a game of cards and then just before midnight, RJ said it was time to make a move. So we all packed ourselves back into the van for our "night out".

CHAPTER 5

The Night Out

Our target for the evening was a big house in the middle of nowhere. RJ said he'd been there a few times and hadn't seen anyone drive in or out through the massive gates. He assured us the house was empty but that security was tight. The only way in was through a small window at the back of the house. Suddenly, everyone began looking in my direction. I was the smallest in the group and the only one who could go through the opening.

I shook my head. I'd never done this before but before I knew what was happening I was being bundled through the window, landing in what looked like a mini church. I had landed in a prayer room. I was terrified, and couldn't move.

RJ kept urging me to open the main door, but I was transfixed. Right in front of me was a huge cross. I remembered Aunt Becca, the church services, the sermons; it all came flooding back. The others began cursing and swearing outside but I was determined not to rob whoever lived in here.

Realizing, however, that I wasn't going to open the door for them, RJ ordered the boys back into the van and drove off, leaving me behind, just as the police were arriving. The owner of the house, an old lady, had spotted me on her bedroom camera and called for help. I stood there shaking as I was handcuffed and led out of the house.

Somehow, the officer in charge knew I was new to the game and decided to give me a warning instead of charging me with a crime. Therefore I didn't have to go to court, much to everyone's surprise. But the school wouldn't have me back so I had to return home.

Aunt Becca was heartbroken. She had emptied her life savings to send me to Harem Comprehensive. I felt really guilty and promised to make it up to her, and the very next day went looking for a job. Unfortunately, no one would hire me. I had no qualifications and everyone knew why I had been sent home from school.

A few weeks later, Aunt Becca suddenly took ill and had to move in with Shirley Blake, a member of the church, who had offered to take care of her. Aunt Becca had babysat every one of Shirley's three children, who were now grown up with families of their own. I was told there was no place for me because the grandchildren often came to stay, but I knew it was because of the robbery. Everyone had lost trust in me.

Aunt Becca had been renting from the government, and her house was soon taken over, so now I had nowhere to live. I begged Aunt Becca's friends to take me in, but they refused. They all knew I had been involved in a stint and feared for their lives and those of their children. The same ones who had welcomed me with open arms some six years earlier would no longer welcome me into their homes.

By now, Aunt Becca had become very weak, so Shirley Blake asked me to return home. I looked at Aunt Becca, hoping for some reassurance, but she simply stared at me. I began to cry. Aunt Becca had become incognitive. But instead of going back home, I headed for the nearest town and was soon knocking on people's doors and asking if they needed help around the house. Rick had always said I wouldn't amount to much, and going home like I was would have only proven him right.

Everything went on well for a while until someone tipped the community that I had been involved in a robbery. That same evening, I was asked to leave and ended up on the streets. I was so angry! I'd been let down and refused the opportunity of a new start.

The only option now was revenge.

One evening, while walking the street, I met one of my old school mates, Dick Singh. He told me they'd all been expelled, and now lived with RJ. I felt a sense of vindication. They'd had their due reward, I thought to myself, not until Dick mentioned that they'd all been looking for me. Apparently, RJ had never been the same ever since I left. I pursed my lips in silence, showing no emotion. I wanted to show that I'd grown and didn't need anyone, but deep within I longed for their company. Dick asked me to come around; gave me the address where they all stayed, then left. "Maybe," I responded casually, putting the address in my coat pocket.

Two days later, I was knocking on RJ's door. The boys came round like a swarm of bees, checking me out, one after the other. They all wanted to know what I'd been up to, but I refused to say much. I wanted to be in control for as long as I could. Then RJ came out of the room, with a huge smile on his face. He told me that he'd missed me, and somehow I knew that was true. I could almost feel the jealousy through the other boys' stares when RJ called me "son", and it felt nice to be loved and appreciated and I lapped up all the attention.

And then RJ asked the boys to give me a burger. I smiled. It was as if he'd read my mind. The burger was huge but I brought it down in no time. Later that evening, RJ asked me to move in with them and I did. And this time, unlike the last, I wasn't afraid to rob anyone, not even an old lady with a huge cross. The church folk had turned their back on me in my hour of need. There was no holding back.

In Frusa, however, Lorna Doe is very worried. She hasn't heard from Becca in months and her letters to Henry haven't been acknowledged either, but she's afraid to travel to Vey, even with a new identity. She's convinced that Rick's out there waiting, not realizing he's been put behind bars. Unfortunately, Becca doesn't have a phone, so now Lorna has no means of gettng in touch with either Becca or Henry.

CHAPTER 6

Living with RJ

My first major assignment after moving in with RJ was a stately home. We'd already been on a few local stints, but I was always put in the background having developed cold feet on a previous assignment. On this occasion, however, I had been put in charge, but on the morning of the raid, I woke up feeling unwell. RJ was very upset. The operation had taken months to plan; there was no turning back, so they left, without me. Sadly, that was the last I saw of anyone of them. The operation went horribly wrong, and RJ was shot, along with the others. It was all in the news.

I was terrified. I knew God was watching over me because shortly after the boys left, I suddenly became well, well enough to follow them, but they'd all switched off their phones so I couldn't contact them. That night I wept; for RJ and for my friends, but more for RJ. He was the father I never had. Very early the next day, before daybreak, I picked up my few belongings and left, but this time, I was determined to make my peace with God.

CHAPTER 7

A New Beginning

The following Sunday, I was in church but not the same one I had attended with Aunt Becca. I wanted a new start with the Lord, and more importantly somewhere no one knew about my dodgy past. The service was great and I enjoyed every minute of it and was soon standing at the altar giving my heart to the Lord.

At the end of the service, one of the deacons offered to give me a ride home but I told him I was homeless. He was shocked but soon arranged for me to stay with one of the single guys in the church. I was welcomed with open arms, given a job taking care of the church, and before long, I was attending evening classes as I tried to complete my secondary school education.

All along I had been thinking of mum but didn't want to go looking for her until I had made something of my life. Not that I knew where she was. Mum had gone to great lengths to hide her new identity and wouldn't disclose where she was or with whom she was staying. I wasn't even allowed to write or phone her in case the calls were intercepted, so everything I wanted to tell her had to go through Aunt Becca, which I thought, was needless, but mum wouldn't have it any other way, so I had to comply.

And now with Aunt Becca being very sick, I simply had no means of getting in touch with my own mother.

Several years later, I was studying Electrical Engineering in college. I had also become a youth leader, and the Bishop's daughter, Carole, had caught my eye.

Carole Nopen was every young man's dream, and every now and then she would drop by at the youth services when she was in town, barely saying a word. I often convinced myself that she'd come round to see me even though she and I hardly exchanged more than a casual greeting.

And then I graduated from college and as I went forward to receive my awards, I spotted Carole in the crowd. My heart skipped a beat, and I almost tripped over, but as I went back to my seat, she was gone. I spent the whole evening analysing the day and wondering if she'd been in attendance, or if my mind had been playing a trick on me.

A few days after graduation, I went back to Vey. I wanted Aunt Becca to know that I had made something of my life. I had my graduation photos and my laminated certificate carefully tucked away in a brown envelope ready for display. Aunt Becca may be unwell, but I was convinced she could decipher what I'd brought with me. But Shirley Blake wouldn't let me in. I bet she thought I still robbed people and feared for her life. So I went back to Yuli, deeply saddened.

A couple of months later, having struck up a friendship with Carole's immediate older brother, Aaron, I decided to ask Carole out, but she turned me down. I was shocked and so was Aaron, who had encouraged me in my pursuit. I almost bailed out of church the following day, in case she'd told everyone. I couldn't bear being made a laughing stock. But I plucked up the courage to attend service as usual and to my surprise, Carole wasn't in the meeting.

I later got to know that she'd attended the early risers' worship service.

Unknown to Henry, Carole Nopen had been seeing Shawn White, a former classmate of hers, in secret. Shawn was a handsome young man, who had all the girls swooning each time he came to church. He was always very polite, helping the women and giving the dads a hand. The mothers liked him too, often asking him to join the family for lunch, but Shawn often charmingly declined with some business excuse always to hand.

CHAPTER 8

Lorna and Adam

*L*orna Doe has just received a letter from her case worker, Amina Sote. Rick has signed off divorce papers, finalizing the process he began years ago. Lorna is over the moon. She's now a free woman.

With that, Lorna begins venturing into the real world once again. She's already gone back to school, but her deepest desire is to reunite with Henry, and with Becca, both of whom she hasn't seen in years. And then a few weeks later, while on a working lunch with Human Rights Lawyer, Adam Locke, Lorna receives a surprise marriage proposal—from Adam. Adam's admired Lorna from a distance—for years—and with Rick now out of the picture, he's keen to make his feelings known. But Lorna is reluctant. Her main concern is to reunite with her son, plus her divorce has only just been finalized. But Adam Locke is soon convincing Lorna to go out with him, and so, the two began dating, with Adam promising to help find Henry.

A few days later, Adam and Lorna are in Vey to see Becca, but Becca hardly recognizes her sister. Lorna is overcome with emotion and begins to cry. She had hoped to use the opportunity to make peace with Becca, especially now that Rick is out of her life for good. Then she asks about Henry, and suddenly Shirley Blake begins shuffling uncomfortably. Lorna and Adam exchange quick glances. They can tell that something isn't quite right. With further questioning, Shirley is soon telling Lorna why Henry no longer lives in the village. Lorna breaks down in tears, crying for the first half of the journey back home.

Six months later, in between searching for Henry and making a living, Adam and Lorna tie the knot, with a couple of their co-workers as witnesses.

CHAPTER 9

Finding Love

In Yuli, however, Carole Nopen has returned to church for the evening service in tears, much to everyone's surprise. Shawn has been arrested for being in possession of drugs at a random police search on their way to a charity event and has confessed not only to dealing drugs but also to taking them.

I stood there transfixed, as Carole sobbed. I wasn't exactly sure of what to say, so I said nothing. That same evening, however, Carole came over to me as I locked up after the service, apologizing for the way she had treated me. I, of course, was more than happy to accept her apology, but decided to play it cool. I didn't want to appear too eager.

Carole Nopen began attending more of our youth services when she was in town and every now and then would stay behind to say "hello" to me. And then one evening, I found her talking to Drake Best, the head Usher, and my heart sank. I'd had a prompting in my spirit to ask her out, the week before, but had hesitated, for fear of being rejected, yet again.

I ran back to my prayer closet and began praying fervently, asking the Lord to bring Carole back and for the boldness to ask her out, and he did. The following day, I went over to Carole and told her that I felt the Lord would have us be together. She broke down crying and almost immediately confessed to having felt the same, but had thought Shawn White was a better option. I knew exactly what she meant. Shawn was a dashing young man, with very strong features, but I wasn't a beast by any chance. My skin was flawless, apart from the mark on my face from one of the many beatings from my step dad, and I had a lovely smile. Everyone said that. Carole then told me how she'd been asking the Lord to bring me back, and yet again, apologized for the way she'd treated me. That made my day.

"And he has," I said, smiling, but deep down I knew the story could have been different, had I not overcome my fear of rejection.

A few days later, I was asking Bishop Craig, Carole's father, if I could date his daughter. I had never felt so nervous in my life even though I had been to their house several times. Bishop Craig had often referred to Carole as his "Princess" and my asking for his permission to date her, I thought, could prove somewhat emotional for him.

The meeting, as I prefer to call it, was less formal than I had expected. Bishop Craig and his wife, Tanya, made me feel at home, smiling broadly as I presented my case. It was almost as if they'd been expecting me to ask Carole out all along, but that didn't stop them from laying some ground rules. Carole and I were to remain pure until our wedding night. Carole and I hugged her father in quick succession. Bishop Craig was a very nice man but was also very unpredictable. He could have easily said, "No", that much I knew, having worked with him for many years. Tanya gave me a big hug and with tears in her eyes, making me promise to look after Carole, whom she said was "the apple of her father's eyes". From then on, Carole and I began dating, and with it came a few jealous stares as we paraded ourselves around town, hand in hand.

A year later, Carole and I were getting engaged in her parent's living room. The Nopens had insisted on an intimate ceremony, so no one outside their immediate family had been invited.

Bishop Craig decided to use the opportunity to counsel me, and I hung onto his every word. Rick hadn't been much of a father, and Brian hadn't stuck around long enough to steer me in the right direction. And RJ, he did his best. He'd never been fathered himself, so had only given me what he could.

As the wedding day drew closer, however, I began having a deep longing to reconnect with my mother. I hadn't heard from her since leaving Vey, but wasn't able to contact her either, as mum had refused to disclose her contact address or phone number, for security reasons. In addition, my Aunt Becca was too sick to leave Vey, which meant I had no one to represent my side of the family, but Bishop Craig assured me I needn't worry. I was now his son.

CHAPTER 10

The Search

Adam and Lorna haven't given up on finding Henry, travelling several miles every weekend in search of the young man. Then one weekend they pulled into a filling station and there standing in the shop was a Brian Bye look-alike. Lorna tries to get a closer look, but the young man was already on his way out.

Lorna Locke pays hurriedly for her fuel, rushes back to the car, and asks Adam to follow the young man's car. She's determined to find out who he is and where he lives.

Some ten minutes later, however, and the young man is heading towards a church building. Adam and Lorna follow him, tenaciously, only to be turned back at the gates. It's a Saturday morning and members of the public aren't allowed into the premises, without prior arrangements. Curious as to the identity of the young man, however, Adam and Lorna decide to fellowship at the church the following day.

Arriving at the service just after 10:00 am, Lorna and Adam are ushered to the front row, much to their delight. "And let's welcome our newcomers," Bishop Craig announces after the opening prayer, with the biggest of smiles, looking at Adam and Lorna.

At that moment, Henry saunters to the stage. "I'm Henry Doe, the Youth Pastor of this great assembly," he says with great conviction, looking at the Lockes. "We're glad to have you fellowship with us and hope you'll make this the first of many visits."

Lorna gasps. She can see the mark on Henry's face where he'd been hit by Rick as a child. "It's him," she whispers excitedly to Adam. "It's my Henry."

Adam flashes his wife a big smile. "Let's wait till after the service, shall we?" He says, quietly nudging Lorna.

Lorna nods hurriedly, but all she can think of is her boy as she waits patiently for the service to end.

The service ends as Bishop Craig comes over to shake hands with Adam and Lorna. Adam pulls him aside. Bishop Craig is somewhat taken aback but keeps his composure. "Can we have a word with you, please?" Adam begins, looking intently at Craig.

"Of course you can. Let's go to my office."

And so Lorna and Adam followed the Bishop to his office.

"So what can I do for you?" Craig asks, looking first at Adam and then Lorna.

"I'm Henry's mother," Lorna says excitedly.

Craig gives Lorna a weird look. Would Henry not have recognized his own mother? He thought to himself, looking suspiciously at Lorna.

"I know you don't believe me, but I really am." Lorna says quietly, bringing out an old photograph of Henry from her purse. "That was Henry just before he left for Vey," she says, lovingly, handing the photograph over to the Bishop.

Craig takes a good look at the photograph but says nothing.

"Here's our hotel address," Lorna tells him, scribbling at the back of her business card. "Please give it to Henry; he can find me there if he wants to see me, and tell him I said my "little warrior boy".

Craig looks into Lorna's eyes. Somehow he could tell that she was telling the truth. "I'll get him for you," he says quietly, grabbing his phone.

A few minutes later, Henry Doe is at the door.

"Our visitors have some news for you," Craig tells Henry as soon as the young man is in his office.

Henry looks intently at Bishop Craig, hoping for some more information, but the Bishop isn't giving anything away. "I'll be in the other room if you need me," he tells Henry, and with that, quietly leaves the room.

"H-e-n-r-y, it's me, Lorna, your mother," Lorna says huskily, getting up to hug her son.

Henry takes a step backwards. Since when did his mother speak with a drawl? And the woman in front of him looked nothing like Lorna.

"I know what you're thinking," Lorna points out, quietly, "but it really is me. I had to reinvent myself after I was rescued from Rick. It's been a very long road to rehabilitation." And with that, Lorna Locke began taking off her "props". First was her wig, then her glasses, and then she began singing "my little warrior boy", the bedtime song she'd made up for Henry when he was five.

Henry gasps and begins to cry. This was his mother, no doubt. No one else could know the warrior song, but her. She'd composed it.

Adam wipes a tear from his face as he watches Lorna and Henry, hugging and crying. It really is an emotional sight.

"And this is Adam, my husband," Lorna says, a few minutes later, as she introduces Henry to Adam Locke.

"Your mother would have left me if we hadn't found you," Adam says jokingly, giving Henry a big hug. "She was always talking about you."

Henry smiles, broadly. He is glad to hear that his mother had often talked about him. "Thanks, for taking care of my mum," he tells Adam. "I can see you've made her very happy."

Lorna looks lovingly at Adam. He sure had made her happy and they were expecting their first child too.

"What about Rick'?" Henry asks eager to know what had become of his step dad.

"The last time I heard, he was in jail, but I don't know if he's been released," Lorna replies, cautiously. "Adam says he can't do anything to me, but Rick has never been one to play by the book, which is why I've still got my 'props'. I don't want to take any chances, not with Rick."

Henry nods. He knew Rick too well.

"Wow! See how you've grown," Lorna exclaims, admiring Henry from every angle. "The last time I saw you, you were hardly up to my waist."

"That was a very long time ago, mum," Henry points out, smiling. "I'm getting married soon, you know."

"Really?! And who's the lucky girl?" Lorna asks, excitedly.

"Bishop Craig's daughter," Henry replies, smugly.

"I see," Lorna returns, poking her son.

"There's a lot more I need to tell you, though," Henry points out, quietly, his left hand anxiously clasped over the right.

"I already know," Lorna replies, pulling her son close. "I've been to Vey. Shirley's told me everything, but I'm glad you've turned your life around."

"Why don't you come to our hotel tomorrow?" Adam suggests. "I'm sure there's a lot more you two need to talk about."

Henry nods in agreement.

"Can we see Bishop Craig before we go?" Lorna asks. "We really need to thank him for giving us an audience."

Craig, of course, is more than happy to have been a part of the family reunion. He's always wanted Henry to reconnect with his mother. "I'm glad I got to play a part in this," he says, happily, giving Henry Doe a pat on the back.

Henry smiles shyly, looking at the floor.

And with that out of the way, the Lockes headed back to their hotel.

Henry Doe stood at the car for several minutes after the Lockes had left, savouring the joy of family. He'd gone from having no one to having a mum, a stepdad, and a little brother or sister on the way—all in one day. He couldn't have asked for more.

The Nopens are equally excited for Henry, but kept the news to themselves. It was up to Henry to break the news to his church family, if and when he wanted to.

The following day, Henry Doe is at the hotel and is soon telling Lorna about his experiences, and how he had ended up with RJ. Lorna sobbed and sobbed, especially after learning that Henry had been refused a place at Shirley's.

Five hours later, however, and Henry is on his way back to Yuli, content and at peace.

CHAPTER 11

The Introduction

A few weeks after their visit to the Church, the Lockes are formally introduced to the Nopens at Henry's request. Craig Nopen is full of praise for Henry, expressing how delighted he is to have the young man court his daughter, while Tanya expresses a deep satisfaction at the way Henry comports himself both in and outside of church.

Lorna Locke feels a huge sense of pride, smiling broadly all through the evening, but deep down she knows she couldn't take the credit for the way her son had turned out. She'd brought Henry into the world, but others had helped raise him.

A couple of months before the wedding, I was in Vey, and this time with Carole. Bishop Craig had suggested taking Carole to see Aunt Becca as she'd played an important role in my life. And this time, Shirley Blake let me in. I think seeing Carole with me had made her realize that I was no longer the person I used to be.

Aunt Becca's face lit up as soon as Carole and I walked into her room. It was almost as if she knew who she was, and before long the villagers were turning up to see us, asking us to stop by their places before leaving for Yuli. But we didn't get a chance to see them all as we had to be back in Yuli for the mid-week service. I left an invite for Aunt Becca and also for Shirley Blake.

CHAPTER 12

Our Wedding

Our wedding day was glorious. Carole looked gorgeous in her flowing white gown. I couldn't believe she was mine and briefly thanked the Lord for removing every obstacle out of the way. By that, of course, I meant Shawn White, especially since learning that he'd never been converted. Carole would have been unequally yoked with an unbeliever, I thought, but I doubt if Shawn would have made it past the Bishop's "surveillance". Bishop Craig's spiritual senses were very sharp or maybe Shawn would have won him over with his charming smile. I, of course, will never know. Not that I cared.

Aaron was my best man, and he did a great job ensuring that I was in church on time, having collected my suit from the dry cleaners a week before the wedding. I had opted for one of my old suits, but it did nicely. Carole and I were determined to start our married life with as little debt as possible. Thankfully, Aaron was able to get the same suit in his size, so we looked like twins, more or less.

Bishop Craig conducted our wedding. He later told me that ours was one wedding he had promised himself to officiate. Mum and Adam sat with Carole's family in the row just behind us. It was really surreal. I'd gone from having no family members to having two, well three, actually (two and one on the way) all in one day. I couldn't have asked for more.

Aunt Becca was also in attendance and even though she hardly said a word, I did feel she was aware of her surroundings, especially after Bishop Craig prayed for her. I saw her face light up briefly as Carole and I waved at the congregation after we'd been pronounced husband and wife. Mum was all smiles, hugging everyone and being all sweet. She'd taken so much to Carole, which made me even happier as I would have hated having to choose between them. They both mean a lot to me. I could already see them shopping together.

The reception was equally great. There was more than enough food and, of course, everyone was keen to know how Carole and I had gotten together. I hid my face briefly behind my champagne flute as Aaron told everyone how I had frantically sought the Lord after Carole hadn't shown up at youth service one Sunday evening. Carole looked at me and smiled. It was the first time she would hear that.

An hour later, I was giving the toast, thanking everyone, and I had a long list. I didn't want to leave anyone out. I was who I was because of these people who believed in me and had given me a second chance, and then we were off on our honeymoon.

CHAPTER 13

My Arrest

It's the first Sunday after our honeymoon. Carole looked beautiful and content as we sat in church. We didn't have much, but we had each other. The service was just about to end when two policemen burst into the church asking for me. One of the ushers pointed to me standing on the podium and before I knew what was happening, I was being led out of the church in handcuffs. Carole slumped on the floor and began to sob. The church was in commotion; no one knew what was happening.

Bishop Craig came outside as I was being taken away, but the police wouldn't give him any more information other than that I had been identified as a suspect in a robbery that took place several years ago. I sat in the police car wondering why this was happening. I'd given my heart to the Lord and was serving Him, wholeheartedly, and yet my past seemed to have caught up with me. Whatever happened to old things has passed away. Why was I being punished for the sins I had committed in my time of ignorance?

Arriving at the station, I was told almost immediately that there was no option of bail. This was one case that had eluded the force for years and they weren't taking any chances in case I "legged it". With that, I was taken away for questioning.

The questioning session had hardly begun when I began to sob, as I suddenly began remembering in detail the very night of the robbery and how I had been pressured into taking part.

It was one of the assignments after I moved in with the boys. Up until then, I'd never used a gun, but RJ told me there was always a first time. He handed me a gun and asked me to shoot a woman at close range as we raided her shop but I was too scared and stood there trembling.

Julius took the gun off me; showed me how it was done, and asked me to do it; "now!" And I did. I fired two shots but missed, but the third one hit the lady and she slumped over. I immediately began emptying her cash box, pulling off my balaclava as I did. And with all her takings for the day stolen, we all filed out of the shop as others made fun of me. That day I made up my mind to improve my aiming skills.

But Helen Tackle, the shopkeeper, had only been playing dead and in a split moment had seen Henry's face as he took off his balaclava and the distinctive lobster tattoo on his left wrist. However, by the time the police arrived, Helen was in such a state of shock and was unable to articulate what she'd seen. Unfortunately, she'd been working alone.

And then a few days later, Helen Tackle was found to have suffered a stroke, unable to remember anything or anyone and with it had gone a huge chunk of her past.

Several years later, Helen Tackle is propped up in bed watching TV when Henry Doe's picture suddenly appears on the screen. Henry has just finished a charity run for his church and is being presented with an award, and as the camera zooms on him, revealing the mark on his face, something resonates with Helen and she starts to scream, and she also spotted the distinctive lobster tattoo on Henry's left wrist.

Judith Tackle comes running into the living room to see her mother trembling and pointing to the TV. And then, Helen starts talking and very quickly, too. She's suddenly remembering the events of the night she was robbed.

Judith grabs her phone and begins recording Helen's every description of the night of the robbery and half an hour later, mother and daughter were at the station.

The police are very delighted to hear Helen's testimony and re-open the case. The very next day Henry Doe is arrested in the church.

Henry Doe begins praying earnestly for God's intervention. He'd done wrong no doubt, but now he needs the mercy of God to prevail on his behalf.

The questioning session is quite brief. Henry cooperates with the police, giving them all the information they want, but the rest of the gang, unfortunately, were no more, so he (Henry) alone would have to face the wrath of the law.

The church becomes divided. Many are getting to know about their Youth Pastor's past and wondering if he should have been appointed in the first place. Over the next few months, Bishop Craig watches his congregation dwindle before his very eyes, as many of his associates begin giving unauthorized interviews to the press.

Then the stories begin to emerge, with one parishioner claiming Henry had been dealing drugs, while another claimed to have seen him at a joint a few days before he was arrested, both of which were false.

But another group prays for Henry's release. The offence had been committed in a time of ignorance, before Henry knew the Lord. They needed the Lord to come through for him, and speedily, too.

CHAPTER 14

Life in Prison

Carole was always at the prison to see me, she'd never missed a day, and then one afternoon, she didn't show up and I began to panic. I'd been in prison for three months and all kinds of thoughts began racing through my mind. Maybe she'd had enough, I thought to myself. I could already see other young men trying to get close to her in my mind and I prayed fervently, asking the Lord to keep Carole safe.

But the enemy kept telling me it was over. I had been told I would be in jail for a very long time. Carole wasn't going to wait for me. And then she showed up, looking drained. I hugged her almost immediately and for a very long time, hardly saying a word. Carole then told me she was pregnant, which was why she hadn't turned up the day before. She had been sick all day. I hugged her yet again. I was to be a dad, but reality soon hit me. What use was a father who was in jail? I sobbed. I didn't want my child growing up without a dad, like I had. I knew Bishop

Craig and Adam would fill in the gap. Mum had already had her baby, a boy, also named Adam and had assured me that she'll take care of mine for me, but I didn't want history repeating itself. I wanted to be there for my son or daughter.

Carole let me sob for as long as I needed to. I think she picked up on why I was crying. However, she told me not to worry as they were praying for me.

And then I had more news. RJ and his boys had been linked to a spate of other robberies, and now I could be in jail for much longer. Apparently, they had witnesses linking me to these other crimes, which had been committed long before I even re-joined the group. I couldn't help but wonder where these "witnesses" had been all along. I needed the Lord's help now more than ever.

Adam and Mum did all they could to get me out of jail, but to no avail. Lorna even wrote a personal letter to the courts, explaining our situation and that I was no longer the person who robbed and stole from people, but was told I still had to stand trial.

From then on, I began to pray and fast asking the Lord to come through for me. I wanted to be around to be a father to my child.

About six months later, Adam came round to see me, and for the first time in months, he had a huge smile on his face. The first thing that came to my mind was that I had become a dad. Carole was close to giving birth and hadn't been to visit for some time. But he told me Helen Tackle had dropped the charges. She'd gotten to know that Carole was expecting our first child and didn't want to deny me the opportunity of seeing my child grow up. I was excited. God was answering my prayers, but then he told me the police still wanted their pound of flesh. They were going for the highest possible sentence for the other robberies. My heart sank. I hadn't participated in these stints, but Adam told me not to worry as he had it all worked out. I was to plead not guilty to these crimes on the ground of diminished responsibility. A friend of his would prepare a report explaining that I'd been suffering from various episodes of psychosis brought on by the abuse I had suffered in childhood. That was bound to get me off the hook, he said.

I thanked Adam for his time and effort but told him I wasn't prepared to lie under oath. Adam was completely taken aback and soon left after that.

The following day, mum came around to visit, and her face said it all. Adam could no longer represent me as I wasn't willing to cooperate with him, she said. I tried to get mum to reason, but she said I was being naïve. Apparently, heaven helps those who help themselves. I wonder where she got that from. She told me to reconsider my stand and left.

That evening, I wrote my son a letter. By now I already knew I was having a boy. I told him how much I loved him, apologizing for the fact that I couldn't be there for his milestones. I told him I had made some very bad choices as a teenager and was now paying for them, which was why I couldn't be there for him. My aim was to give the letter to Carole when she came to visit the next time.

CHAPTER 15

My Trial

It's the day of Henry's trial. Bishop Craig and his prayer team have been sitting in the courtroom for an hour and a half, holding hands and praying under their breath. Lorna and Adam sit directly behind them, looking apprehensive. They'd heard that the police chief was planning to make Henry an example. Apparently, one of his cousins had been shot during one of RJ's raids and though he survived, had been traumatized ever since.

Half an hour later, Henry Doe is brought in looking very pale, and without any legal representation. The proceedings begin, with the prosecutor being asked to call forward his witnesses. Suddenly all goes quiet. There are no witnesses, not a single one.

There are murmurings in the courtroom as people begin looking around to see what is going on. The prosecuting lawyer looks flustered. Walking up to the judge, he asks for more time to confer with his team, and with that, the hearing is adjourned till the afternoon.

The hearing is resumed, but there are still no witnesses, not a single one. The prosecuting lawyer tries to come up with an excuse, but the Judge has had enough and without any hesitation throws the case out of court. Henry Doe is now a free man.

There are shouts of jubilation from the church members who had sat in the gallery. Henry falls on his knees in the dock and thanks the Lord for sparing his life. Lorna runs forward to hug her son and so does Adam who is so shocked that he's unable to speak. He'd been told that the case against Henry was so strong that a prison sentence was inevitable. His Barrister friend, Joe Tan, is even more shocked. He's never attended a court session where none of five witnesses turn up in court. What a huge embarrassment this was to the prosecutors!

Carole Doe is already in the early stages of labour when one of the nurses comes rushing in to share the good news. A friend of hers had been in court and had seen Henry being acquitted. Suddenly Carole is fully dilated, and before anyone knew what was happening, baby Joshua had crowned. The midwife throws her phone in mid-air and is soon helping Carole deliver her baby boy as Tanya watches with utmost pride. She's now a grandmother, and the delivery has only lasted half an hour.

CHAPTER 16

The Plot

Unknown to Henry and everyone else, the "witnesses" had all been paid to say they'd seen Henry Doe pull the fatal trigger that had hit Dennis Van, the Chief Inspector's cousin, even though no gun had been found.

But a couple of days before the trial, Gary Page, the key witness had called the police to say he wanted out. He'd known no peace ever since he got paid to be a witness and was willing to return every penny. However, he was told it was too late. He had to appear in court or face the wrath of the police. The other four witnesses had simply disappeared without a trace.

A few days later, it was all in the news. Gary Page had gone to the press and sold his story. The officer in charge denies the allegation, but alas Gary has recorded their conversation on his phone. The officer resigns almost immediately, but is determined not to go down alone, and is soon implicating Chief Inspector Van, who is equally charged to court.

And then the press comes knocking at the Nopen's where Henry had been staying following his release from prison. They wanted a story, but Henry Doe politely declined. He'd been acquitted and that was all that mattered, he'd told them. But Bishop Craig encouraged Henry to tell his story, because if he didn't others would, and sure enough, they did.

With everyone wanting their two minutes of fame, all sorts of stories begin appearing in the press, most of them a repetition of what someone else had said.

And so Henry Doe tells his story, with particular emphasis, however, on how he'd come to know the Lord. The story sells very well and the church is soon holding three services back to back as people began trooping in to see Henry and to hear his story.

Many of those who come end up giving their hearts to the Lord and soon began attending the church. Adam and Lorna also give their hearts to the Lord during one of their many visits to the church.

And that was the beginning of my ministry as I began travelling around the world, with my beautiful wife, of course, reaching out to young boys and men, and encouraging dads to be true fathers indeed.

For that which the enemy meant for evil,
the Lord turned around for good.

Echoes From the Past –
A young man's search for love and identity

Rick Doe returned to his homeland of Nuz after he was released from prison. He also gave me the option of changing my surname from Doe, the surname I'd taken up after he adopted me, to any other name I wanted, but I chose to keep his name. It's a subtle reminder of how far the Lord has brought me.

Brian Bye, my natural father, contacted me again after twenty years, wanting a relationship with me, but never showed up on the day we arranged to meet. And Aunt Becca; she passed away at the ripe old age of ninety-five, having miraculously recovered from her illness, some eighteen years prior.

Acknowledgements

A massive "Thank you" to my family. You make everything worthwhile. Thank you so much for allowing me to be me.

To Ebbie, my dear friend; you are such an encourager. Thank you.

And to my heavenly Father, the creator of the universe, "Thank you" for making me who I am, and for the opportunity to show the world that you care.

This book is dedicated to all the **_"Henry Does"_** of our time.